The Diary of a Rubbish Witch

The Big Move

Natalie Bailey

The Diary of a Rubbish Witch

Crazybirds Publishing.

Book design by Natalie Bailey

For my wonderful husband – thank you for always believing in me.

Being a witch is cool, right? Wrong! Being a witch is only cool if you're any good at it. Me? I'm an awful witch. No – worse than that, I'm absolutely useless. My name is Georgie Mills and I'm eleven years old. I live with my family and yes, they're all witches too. My dad is superb at witchcraft, but he only ever uses his powers when he has to; he's far too busy pretending to all of the outside world that he's completely 'normal'. My mom is brilliant at casting multiple spells at the same time and with a click of her fingers she can make beds, wash the dishes, dust the furniture and get dressed – all at the same time! My older sister Sophia is a natural when it comes to all things witchy and boy – does she know it! She's showing all of the promise of becoming an amazing witch and can cast a spell without a seconds thought. Then there's me – rubbish! I'm not even kidding.

I can't do anything right - even when I try really, really hard. My spell bottles are all empty because I have no idea how to mix potions and my cauldron is filled to the brim with teddy bears because there's no point using it for anything else. Every evening me and Sophia sit at the kitchen table, while mom teaches us the art of being a witch. Sophia makes notes in her notepad like a complete swat and she only has to be shown how to do something once and that's it - it's stuck in her big, clever, show-off brain. I make notes too but I can't keep up with her. Somewhere along the line I jot down the wrong ingredient or spell a word incorrectly, and when it's my turn to practice, things either blow up or disappear completely! Mom looks at me sympathetically, but I can't help but feel that she's slightly disappointed in my lack of ability. Sophia couldn't be sympathetic if she tried, and is all too quick to bask in my failings; she's so annoying!

It's frustrating for me because it's not as if I'm not trying my best but it doesn't make a difference; my best is never quite good enough. Usually, I can talk about everything to my best friend Beth, but I'm not going to be able to do that anymore now that we're moving house again.

We're not just moving to a new house but to a new town too. It's all my mom's fault (AGAIN!!!) because she lost her temper (AGAIN!!!). It's not that my mom is a cruel or wicked woman, she's actually quite nice but when someone is mean to her, her natural witch instincts force itself out and she casts a spell before she has time to stop herself. My family spends more time pretending that we're not witches than we do actually being witches. Unfortunately, people are still frightened of witches; it completely freaks them out. When people discover that me and my family are witches, they either completely blank us because they think that we're going to turn them into frogs or something (get real!).

Rarely do crowds of outraged townspeople surround our house with flaming torches and pitchforks – but it has happened a couple of times! The easiest thing for us to do is to just pack up and move on, which is a shame in this instance because I really liked living in the town we're in now. If it wasn't for mom, then we'd still be living here and I'd still have my friend Beth. Well, to be fair if it wasn't for Mrs Martin and her horrible, snide comments then I'd still have my friend. Mrs Constance Martin has always hated our family. I think she's a little bit jealous of my mom because she's quite pretty (for a grown-up) whereas Mrs Martin actually looks more like a witch than we do. She has a large, crooked nose with a big fat wart on the end of it and her front tooth is missing owing to an unfortunate event at the cricket club last summer (a cricket ball was blasted into the crowd at about 100mph!) Anyway, Mrs Martin and mom got into a little bit of an argument at the hairdressers when mom took me to see if they could do anything with the big fuzz-ball that was my hair.

"I don't know why you're worried about Georgie's hair," Mrs Martin had said with a sly grin. "It's yours that could do with some attention. It looks as though a bird has just set up home on the top of your head."

Everyone is scared of Mrs Martin and so she's used to getting away with saying such nasty things. But my mom isn't scared of anyone. I watched as her face initially went crimson with embarrassment as the other ladies in the hairdressers sniggered around us. Then mom's complexion went from crimson to red with rage, and I closed my eyes and waited for the inevitability of mom's response.

"Are you saying that my hair looks like a birds nest?" she asked Mrs Martin bluntly.

Mrs Martin looked shocked that anyone had dared to answer her back. "I didn't say that exactly, but it does look a little wild – wouldn't you say so my dear?" she replied, sarcasm heavy in her tone.

Mom walked straight up to Mrs Martin and stared directly into her eyes. I shuddered, I'd seen the look on mom's face several times in my life; it was the stare that a mom makes when all kids know that they mean business!

"Actually no, I wouldn't say so," said mom. "In actual fact I'd say that THIS looks more like a birds nest."

Mom swished her finger in the air and pointed to the top of Mrs Martin's head. I squirmed in my seat as Mrs Martin's long, sleek hair was transformed into a large, round, twiggy-nest – complete with birds.

And not just any birds. Oh no – they were American Bald Eagles; who it seemed, didn't much like they're new surroundings and proceeded to flap and squawk around Mrs Martin's head. Mrs Martin flayed her arms wildly and tried to fend off the attacking eagles, and screamed her way straight out of the hairdressers. Funny? - Yes. Deserved? - Absolutely. But it pretty much sealed my family's fate – the look on everyone's faces in the shop told me that. We knew that that sort of information would spread like wildfire in a small town like ours. It wouldn't be long before the whispers started, or for people to start ignoring us as if we weren't there. So there was no other option for us, but to move. Here we go again!

26th December – 11:40am

Aunt Victoria visited today with Christmas presents for me and Sophia. I usually dread receiving gifts from Aunt Victoria – it's not because I'm ungrateful or anything like that, but she always tends to buy us clothes which are generally;

*Too big

*Of the knitted variety (complete with hideous animal motif)

* Something that I wouldn't be seen dead in. In fact if I dropped down dead tomorrow and had nothing else to be buried in – then I'd rather wear my dressing gown!

So it came as a little bit of a surprise when Aunt Victoria hands me a small rectangular box, wrapped in a beautiful snowflake paper and a tied neatly with a big blue bow.

It was apparent that this gift was not going to be another vile piece of clothing and I tried to hide my excitement as I untied the bow, unfolded the paper and lifted the lid off the box. There, covered in a thin piece of tissue paper was the most beautiful book I had ever seen; a diary in actual fact. Large, beautifully illustrated butterflies emblazoned the cover.

I flick through the pages and was pleased to find that each page also bore the faint outline of butterflies on the paper. I ran up to Aunt Victoria and squeezed her tightly and then ran upstairs to my bedroom and sat at my desk. I had never kept a diary before – I suppose there didn't seem much point when I was younger. Now though, everything is different, because in two days' time we'll be moving and I won't have Beth to talk to anymore.

2:30 PM

It's packing time! I know what you're all thinking - 'they've left a bit late haven't they?', but your forgetting one simple thing, we're witches remember? Mom has been teaching me and Sophia a simple packing spell for a few days and now it's time for a trial run.

"Now what I want you to do girls," she says to Sophia and me, "is use your powers to move these items from the kitchen table and straight into the cardboard box."

On the table was;

One of dad's workshirts.

A toothbrush

Three books

And a pencil case

Mom gives us a quick demonstration and with a flick of her wand I watch as the items lift off the table and float with ease, straight to the cardboard box.

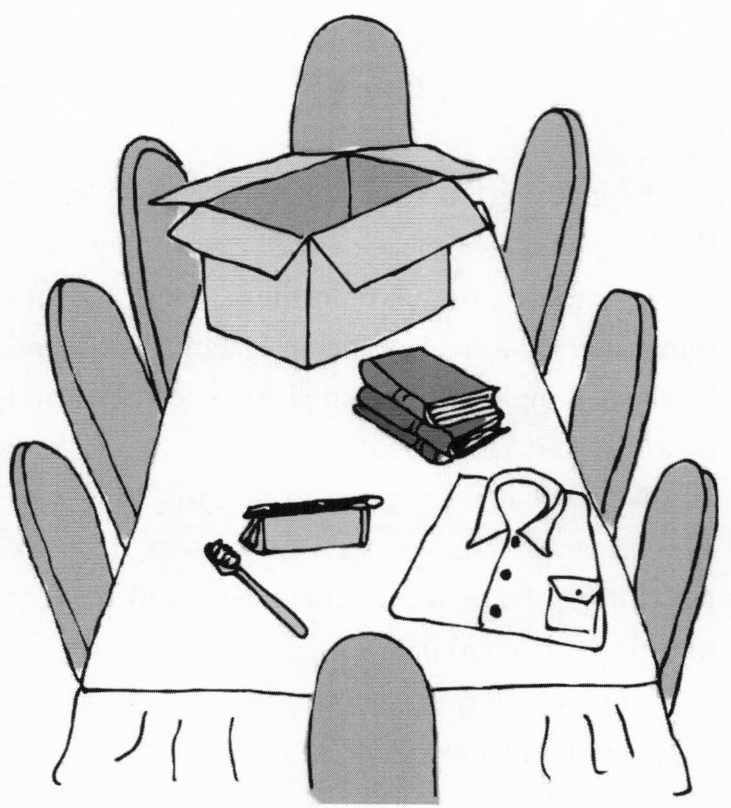

"Right your turn first," she says to Sophia as she uses her magic to empty the box again.

Sophia sighs and rolls her eyes. "Mom, this is sooooo easy! Why do I have to practice?" she says with such self-assurance that I want to throw my wand at her.

"Because you do – now just get on with it!" says mom impatiently.

Sophia huffs again and waves her wand. Once again the things lift from the table and straight into the cardboard box.

"Good girl," says mom, speaking to Sophia as though she was a baby. "You should have no trouble with packing your things. Go on – off you go while I carry on with Georgie."

A smug grin spreads across Sophia's face and my stomach lurches. "No, I think I'll stay and watch Georgie have a go – just to make sure that I completely understand it."

All of a sudden I feel under a great deal of pressure. Sophia is only staying because she wants to see me mess up – again. Not that mom thinks that for a moment.

"Good idea," she replies, not realising the real reason for Sophia's sudden interest in learning. "Right Georgie, I'm ready when you are."

I slowly lift my wand and hesitate. I look over to Sophia who is watching me with her arms folded. I flick my wand the way mom did and to my horror the whole kitchen table begins to lift off the floor!

Mom rushes to my side. "No, no, no. Not the table Georgie, just the things on it," she says - as if I didn't know that already.

A trickle of sweat runs down the side of my face as I attempt to focus clearly.

"Concentrate Georgie, you can do this," mom whispers in my ear.

The table gently lowers back to the ground. I narrow my eyes and stare hard at the things on the table and to my relief and to be perfectly honest – amazement, they began to lift and hover in the air.

Mom claps her hands with joy. "See! I knew that you could do it," she squeals.

"Yeah," says Sophia, with a hint of annoyance. "Now, you've just gotta put them in the box."

Stupid Sophia, I think to myself as I attempt to concentrate back on my spell casting. She loves it when things go wrong for me.

"Concentrate Georgie," says mom as our possessions start to shake gently in the air.

There she is little miss wonderful, just waiting for me to mess up.

"You're need to fix your attention entirely on them," mom says to me, as the shaking intensifies. "Clear your mind, don't think about anything else."

Easy for you to say, you haven't got someone's eyes burning into your back, willing you to fail. God – why did

I have to have a sister? I would have loved to have been an only child. She's such a know-all!

"Georgie, you're still not focusing."

Maybe if she was kinder to me, I might be able to cast spells better?

"Georgie," says mom.

There she is, with her perfect hair and perfect skin and perfect wand!

"Tut. Oh dear," says Sophia. "You'd better stick to the traditional way and pack your suitcases by hand."

Instantly enraged, the volatile items which were shaking like they were in an invisible earthquake – fly straight to the thing I was focused on; namely – Sophia!

“Arrghhhh,” she screams as the books bounce off her head. “What do you think you’re doing? Are you some kind of moron?”

“Sophia!” bellows mom in my defence but I could tell from her face that she too, is frustrated with the lack of my ability. I throw my wand across the kitchen and run to my bedroom.

2:45 PM

My sister is an idiot !!!

27th December 10:00 AM

I spent all of yesterday evening trying to do the stupid packing spell – result? I managed to pack three hair bobbles, one shoe and my pyjamas! That alone took me almost three hours. I just couldn't hold the spell for long enough to get my things into the boxes. I dropped so much on the floor that in the end mom came up to my room to see what I was up to (I think she thought that I was still in a mood because of what happened in the kitchen).

"You ok Georgie?" she asks as she poked her head around my door. "Listen, don't be downbeat about it all. It takes years of practice to be able to cast without any problems."

"But Sophia has no problem at all when she does it, and she's only three years older than me!" I retort as I plonk myself down on my bed.

Mom sits down next to me and places her arms around my shoulder. "How about we give it another shot? Right now – just you and me."

I was more than a little reluctant to attempt the packing spell again. I'd already managed to concuss my big sister (although that wasn't a bad thing I suppose), but the fact that I'd struggled still when I was alone in my room, didn't fill me with belief of success. On the other hand - mom was here to help and it wouldn't hurt to try one more time? I mean what could possibly go wrong? I nod and jump off the bed with a renewed enthusiasm.

"Right. Let's try packing your……" Says mom as her eyes scan the bedroom for what is most likely the easiest thing for me to levitate with my powers, "…your teddies," she says as her eyes settle on my cauldron.

"No problem," I reply with confidence. "Easy-peasy!"

I'm not sure who I was trying to convince – probably mom. I'd failed to pack a toothbrush earlier so didn't hold out much hope for the teddies, but I reasoned that with mom there to guide me, I stood a good chance of being able to actually pack my cuddly friends away.

"Now concentrate on the teddies," says mom.

I stare hard at them all, which was a bit weird because it makes me look like I want to start a fight with them. No! I must stop my mind wandering, this is why I'm never able to complete a spell. I turn my stare into a glare and slowly lift my wand in their direction. I see a slight movement as the teddies shake ever so gently. My spirits are immediately lifted – the spell seems to be taking effect already! Mom see's that I'm pleased with myself and continues to whisper words of encouragement in my ear.

"That's it – well done Georgie! Now what you need to do now is think about them lifting into the air. Go on – you can do it."

I focus my mind on the levitation part. Mom's right – I can do this! The teddies begin to shake more and more and I watch them rise.

"Just the teddies Georgie," says mom as we both realise that I'm also managing to levitate the cauldron too.

I start to panic and concentrate on landing the cauldron on the ground again but it won't work, and in my frustration it begins to sweep around the bedroom.

"Help me!" I scream to mom, who leaps down onto the floor to avoid being hit by the flying iron pot.

"I can't," she shouts back at me. "I left my wand downstairs."

Now I really am in trouble – the only reason I agreed to do this was because I thought that if things did go wrong, mom would be able to help me out.

"You're going to have to do this yourself," says mom, much to my horror. "CONCENTRATE"

Mom was getting angry now - I was just plain scared. I had no choice but to carry on. I look at the cauldron which is still sweeping around the room. I point my wand and think – hard. I see the cauldron in my mind and keep thinking and thinking and thinking…..until.

"You've stopped it flying!" exclaims mom with relief.

My cauldron had indeed stopped spinning through the air and was now motionless, hovering near the ceiling.

Mom jumps back up. "All you have to do now is land it," she says quietly.

I nod and with my wand still pointing at the cauldron, I narrow my eyes and fix my attention on landing the wretched thing safely back on the ground. Nothing happens.

"No darling," says mom with a slight edge of irritation in her voice. "Land it – just see the cauldron gently lowering to the floor."

I nod again and adopt the same squinty-eyed, angry glare at the cauldron. I'm focus so strongly that my wand begins to shake in my hands. Still nothing.

"Georgie – Lower it!"

I stand and stare.

"You can do it my girl," says mom.

I'm still staring, gripping my wand so tightly that I feel it might snap at any moment.

"Put it on the floor – now!" mom says loudly, unable to conceal her frustration any longer.

"I CAN'T!" I scream back, breaking my focus and lowering my wand.

Mom gasps and we both look at the cauldron which, for a brief moment continues to hover in the air – before falling back to the ground and crashing straight through the floor and into the living room below.

10:15 AM

After the cauldron careered through the floorboards mom and I peeped through the gaping hole it had left.

There was dad sat in his armchair, reading the newspaper and looking a little alarmed to say the least. Covered in debris and dust, dad's mouth was agape as he stared at the cauldron which had landed straight on top of the coffee table. At that moment Sophia came into view and looked up at me and mom through the hole.

"Wow! Just when I thought you couldn't get any worse at casting, you go and prove me completely wrong."

The pleasure on her face was clear and anger bubbled away inside me as a big, fat, stupid grin spread across her face. Mom was too busy looking at the state of her house to notice me accidently (on purpose) flick a little dust straight onto Sophia's face below. She coughed and spluttered before making a hasty exit – good job too, because the next thing I had to hand to throw at her was a lump of floor-joist!

16:00 PM

The brick-by-brick repair spell is seriously impressive! After my little 'accident', mom and dad cast the spell together – intensifying the magic. Within seconds, lumps of wood, nails and bits of plaster lifted from the floor in the living room and returned to the ceiling. All of the cracks in the plaster sealed over as if they were never there in the first place and within minutes the hole had been repaired. For good measure, mom then cast a spic-and-span spell and the vacuum whirred around our feet as the polish and duster flitted across the furniture.

"There you go. It's like it never happened," says dad as he picks up his newspaper and settles back in his armchair.

"Right – let's go and finish packing up your room then," mom says to me.

Sophia gasps and grabs mom by the arm. "You're not going to let her," her head nods in my direction, "loose with her wand again, are you?"

"Stop being so horrid Sophia," replies mom as she tugs her arm out of Sophia's grasp. "We all make mistakes."

"Yeah but mine have never resulted in a whacking great hole in the ceiling," Sophia retorts.

A rolled-up newspaper floats over to Sophia and smacks her on the back of the head."

"Ow!!" says Sophia with surprise.

"Don't answer your mother back," says dad as the newspaper floats back towards him, uncurls and opens back up to the page that dad was last reading.

Sophia huffs and storms from the room and mom and I head back upstairs to my bedroom.

"I do think…," starts mom, before pausing.

I knew where this conversation was heading. Mom thought Sophia was right – that I shouldn't pack – well, not with magic anyway.

"You think that you should do my packing for me?" I say, trying not to sound too resentful.

"Well….it's just that, it all has to be done by the end of today. Tomorrow is our last full day here and I really don't want to be rushing about. I want to enjoy every last moment here before Monday comes."

Mom's words hit me. It was our last day tomorrow! I drop onto my bed and nod solemnly at mom.

"Don't look so glum," she says to me, concerned. "Our next house is one of those big, beautiful gothic looking ones that you love so much and who knows – you might make even more friends at your next school?"

I scoff. Even more friends! That shouldn't be too hard considering that I only had one friend here. But she wasn't just any friend – she was my best friend. Mom rubs my shoulder, the discussion it seemed, was over. I continue to sit on my bed, dumbstruck and watch as mom expertly cast the packing spell and my whole life is yet again, packed away into cardboard boxes.

28th December – 6.30 AM

I'm awake at 6.30am! I'm never awake at 6.30am. I know why I'm up though – today is the last day in this beautiful house and try as I might, I can't sleep any longer. I don't want to waste a single minute of today. I want every second to be spent walking around each room, touching the walls and looking out of the windows.

I get out of my bed and slip on my dressing gown – the house feels chilly; draughts of cold winter air, creep in through the old air-vents and brickwork. I pull my dressing gown tightly around me creep downstairs. I can hear movement in the kitchen already, I hope it's not Sophia!

Thankfully it isn't Sophia, it's mom and dad. They haven't noticed me standing in the doorway watching them. They're chatting about what the plan is going to be when the removal men turn up tomorrow morning.

"I wish we could just use our magic to load the vans," says mom. "We'd be done in no time!"

"Yes, but that would defeat the whole point of us moving in the first place," replies dad. "The first thing the removal men would do is gossip their way all over the new town and before you know it, we'd have another witch hunt on our hands."

"We could always just stay," I say from place in the doorway, making mom and dad jump with surprise. "We could just ride it out and see how it goes here?"

Mom walks over to me and crouches down, looking me in the eyes. "Oh my darling," she says to me softly. "I wish it were that easy but you have no idea how vicious and horrible some people can be. We'd never be able to live freely if everyone knew what we really were."

I knew mom was going to say something like that. I want to cry but I don't – there's no way that I'm going to ruin my last full day here. Without saying another word I leave the kitchen and go back to my room.

13:30 PM

I'm lying on my bed. My bedroom is a mass of cardboard boxes. The shelves are empty. The doors of my wardrobe and drawers of my dressing table are open, exposing the emptiness within – it looks like we've been burgled.

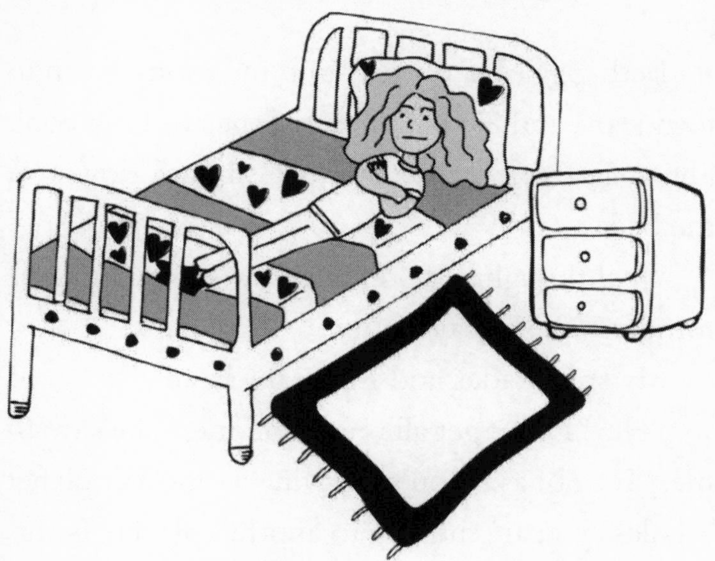

There's a gentle tapping on my bedroom door. I ignore it – I'm not in the mood to speak to anyone; I might pretend to be asleep. The knocking continues as does my refusal to acknowledge whoever the mystery 'tapper' is. The handle starts to turn – how rude! Can a girl not get any privacy in this house? I look around for the nearest object to throw but all of my things have been safely packed away in the boxes.

"You awake?" says Beth's voice from the small opening in the doorway.

I smile and sit up. "I'm never asleep if it's you."

Beth giggles and walks into my room. Even in torn jeans and T-shirt, she manages to look cool. She gives me a big hug and we sit back down on the bed.

"Just thought I'd pop in and wish you luck for tomorrow," she says to me.

My smile fades and I bow my head.

"Hey! Don't get all mushy on me," she says to me. "It's not as if you're moving to another planet – unless you are moving to another planet? Is this some sort of witchy thing that you do?"

I laugh and shake my head. "No of course not," I reply. "But it's not going to be the same is it? We won't be able to just pop in to each other's houses whenever we feel like it, will we?"

Beth sighs and leans back on her arms. "No of course not, but we're not living in the dark-ages anymore," she says to me.

"What do you mean?"

"Well, I may not be able to invade your home in person anymore but there is such thing as emails and if you ever get with the times – Skype!"

"It's not quite the same though is it? Talking to you over a computer screen," I reply.

"Nope – but it's the only thing we've got for now."

I look at my friend and admire her ability to find the positive in every situation that she's faced with. "I suppose we won't be young forever, we'll be able to meet up when we're a little older."

"Exactly, and don't forget the school holidays either. Trust me, you won't be able to get rid of me," she replies.

We spend the rest of the afternoon chatting and giggling, and before we know it hours have passed. I look over at Beth, who is busy impersonating Mrs Cragnall - the school secretary (she's doing quite an impressive job of it too), and I wonder if our friendship will still be the same when I've gone.

17:00 PM - Dinnertime

The sky outside has changed from a depressive winter grey to pitch-black, and mom was calls us down for dinner. Me and Beth head straight down the stairs - all of that chatting is hungry work. The kitchen table has been laid with placemats, cutlery and glasses but there's no food to be seen.

Beth's eyes light up. "Great, it's a witchy dinner!" she says happily.

Beth had known for some time that my family were witches and instead of feeling afraid, she found our abilities fascinating. I wish everyone would see us the way she did.

"I thought we could have a treat, seeing as it's our last day," says mom. "Wands at the ready!"

We all take out our wands as Beth watches on.

"Chicken tikka masala," says Dad.

"Barbeque spare ribs and egg-fried rice," says Mom.

"Cheeseburger and fries," says Sophia.

I looked over at Beth. "Fish, chips and peas for me please," she says.

Yum – that sounded good to me too. "Fish, chips and peas – twice."

Together, we all flick out our wands and point them on the centre of the table. A bright flash of light blares out, causing us to close our eyes; when we open them again we see that the table is heaving with food.

Dad's chicken tikka masala is steaming on a plate in front of him. Mom's barbeque spare ribs are stacked high on a top of a mountain of rice. Sophia's cheeseburger is the size of the dinner plate itself and the fries line the edge of the plate like a moat. Then there was mine and Beth's dinner; I'd asked for fish, chips and peas twice, and that is exactly what we got – two fish, two chips and two peas.

Sophia, predictably bursts out laughing and had I had more chips on my plate, I would have thrown them at her big, smug face. I look over at Beth who is also in a fit of giggles and soon even mom and dad start to chuckle along too. I sit there and even though I've managed to mess up yet another spell, my incompetence on this occasion, makes me smile and in the end I'm laughing uncontrollably with the rest of my family and Beth.

29th December – 8:30AM

Well today is the day! The house is pretty much packed up and we're just waiting for the removal guys to arrive. Considering I was so upset at us having to move again, Beth managed to put a positive spin on at all and our last evening together had been spent joking and laughing. I didn't even cry when I gave her a big squeeze at the end of the night (Beth doesn't do tears – they're for wimps apparently!). I feel a little disloyal to admit that there is a slight part of me that is actually looking forward to seeing what our new home is like. I'm sort of hoping to make friends easily – lots of them with any luck. But what I'm really hoping is that we settle in this place and that don't have to move again, which I'm sure we won't have to – if mom can keep her temper in-check that is.

10:30 AM

The removal men have just turned up and are busy hoisting our furniture onto their van. Mom is loitering around them, making sure that they're not bashing our stuff into the doorframes as they take it out the house. I know it's killing her not being able to just use her powers to load the van. I'm in my room giving it a final sweep, making sure that I haven't accidently left anything behind. I have – three odd socks and two dried-up colouring pens; nothing important.

1:30 PM

The van is loaded and we're on our way. Dad locked up the house for the final time but he didn't seem at all phased or emotional about it – suppose he's used to it by now. We all cram into our car, which is also packed to the rafters with boxes and suitcases.

Sophia is sprawled out on the back seat, leaving me about five inches of seat to squeeze on; she's busy texting away on her phone and seems not to notice my huffing and sighing next to her.

"Ready guys?" says Mom. "Say bye to the old house."

Sophia rolls her eyes, clearly she's far too cool to do something so babyish. I look out of the window and take one last look – I don't say goodbye (I can be cool too sometimes!). I just discreetly wave at the house in a way that no one can see (Ok – maybe not that cool).

17:15 PM

Well it feels like we'd been traveling for eternity but we're finally here. Mom was right about the house – I do love it! It's big, dark and creepy looking and is a cross between the houses of the Addams family and the Munsters.

Me and Sophia rush out of the car and straight to the door, it's a ritual that we do each and every time we move house – the choosing of the bedrooms! The fastest lays claim to the best bedroom and it's a race that I always, always, always lose.

Mom deliberately takes her time to get out of the car and to the front door with the house keys which only heightens our excitement. I make a silent vow to myself that this year – whatever the costs, I am going to get the best room!

Slowly mom unlocks the door and as far as me and Sophia are concerned, the green light has been given and we're off like a shot. Sophia shoulder-barges me out of the way and I almost faceplant straight into an imposing wooden bannister on the stairs.

"You wanna fight dirty?" I shout at her, but she just laughs and bounds up the stairs.

"What other way is there?" she bellows back at me.

I use all of my energy and rush up quickly behind and grab her by one of her ankles and she falls flat on her stomach. I jump over her and continue towards the bedrooms, Sophia is still sprawled on the floor and for once I feel victorious. But my euphoria is short-lived and before I know it, I too fall face-first onto the floor. Sophia walks up towards me as I'm rub my nose and I spy that she's got her wand in her hand. Looking down at my feet, I see that my shoelaces have tied together and I look back at my sister with dismay.

"You cheated! We never use magic – that's against the rules."

Sophia shrugs. "The rules are that I always win little sis and don't you forget it." My nose hurts and suddenly I don't feel in the mood to play this game of 'bag the best bedroom' anymore. Anyway, if Sophia is using magic there's not much point.

"Argh – this is the one for me," I hear Sophia say from one of the empty rooms, before she comes into view again and closes her new bedroom door in my face.

I rub my nose again and sigh with defeat as I untie my shoelaces. I wander around the rest of the rooms. There's one with an ensuite bathroom (that's definitely for mom and dad, so there's no point even trying to stake a claim on it) another bedroom which overlooks the side of the house and one tiny bedroom which is the size of a small cupboard!

"Wow – what a varied choice I have," I mutter beneath my breath.

"What's wrong?" asks mom, who's snuck up behind me.

I sulkily fold my arms across my chest. "As usual, Sophia won the best bedroom and I'm left the mind-blowing choice between these two," I say pointing to the two spare rooms.

Mom looks at the 'cupboard' bedroom and confusion washes over her face. "That's a linen store Georgie, not a bedroom."

"But I thought you said that this house has four bedrooms?" I ask, equally confused.

Mom nods. "It does – the fourth room is on the second floor. I'm surprised that Sophia didn't choose that one!"

I gasp and rush around the corridor, flinging open all of the doors as I hunt for the one which leads to the next floor. I find it, and rush up another flight of stairs and straight into the biggest room I have ever seen in my life. It's as big as all of the rooms below put together, and had windows on the each side of the house.

I let out a squeak of joyous excitement as I scan my new room and spin around deliriously with my arms outstretched – just because I can! I stop spinning and see Sophia standing in my doorway with a very sour and cross look on her face.

"It's not fair!" she screams. "This should be my room, I didn't even know it was here."

Mom shouted up the stairs at her. “It is fair Sophia – you chose the room down here. If you weren’t so hell-bent on beating your little sister you’d have probably had it too!”

I walk up to my door as my big sourpuss of a sister watches on grumpily. “Argh – this is the one for me,” I say, mimicking Sophia’s earlier words to me and slam the door in her face.

19:45 PM

It took the removal men over two hours to unload all of our things; we waved them off and it took mom and dad around twenty minutes to unpack everything into their rightful place. The house feels instantly homely with our familiar possessions around us. Sophia is still sulking about my bedroom, not that mom and dad have taken any notice of her. I'm still reeling with happiness because for once, I won.

"I'm pooped," I say with a yawn to my parents. "I'm off to bed."

"Night love," mom and dad reply.

"Enjoy your room," says Sophia with bitterness, which only makes me feel even better about myself.

In my bedroom, I begin to close the blinds at the windows. At the window, I notice a figure in the window of the house opposite. It's another girl but it's sort of difficult to tell, as apart from a small gap, her hair pretty much covers her entire face.

We continue to stare at each other and I'm beginning to feel slightly awkward, so I raise my hand and wave over at the stranger. She looks away as though embarrassed and quickly raises her hand, waves back before closing the curtains quickly.

"Weird!" I whisper.

I don't dwell on my new next door neighbour too much, I'm far too tired and before long, I'm tucked up in my warm, soft bed and fall into a deep sleep.

30th December 11:15 AM

The great thing about old houses is that you can find all sorts of quirky and wonderful hiding places. During my detailed exploration I have found a secret compartment behind a panel in my closet, a small nook nestled in between the floorboards on the landing, a roomy space behind the bath panel and small hidey-hole behind the panelling in the study. Superb!

I wrap up and decide to go outside and have a mooch in the garden. As gardens go, this one is impressive -and I'm not a fan of gardens at all. The mature trees and shrubs provide ample privacy from the neighbouring houses and the way in which the flowerbeds wind around the garden, you get the sense that it will look really beautiful and picturesque in spring and summertime. It seems to go on for miles too and as I walk deeper into the bushes towards the end, I find a small clearing where a rickety-old shed stands, next to which is a small round table and two wonky chairs.

"Psst."

I jump round, alarmed – crikey, I hope there aren't any snakes here!

"Psst. Over here."

I walk behind the shed and see a small hole in the dividing fence behind. An eyeball suddenly fills the hole and nearly wet myself with fright.

"Argghhhhhh," I scream.

"Be quiet – otherwise they'll here you," says the voice.

I immediately crouch to my knees and crawl closer to the hole. "Who will?"

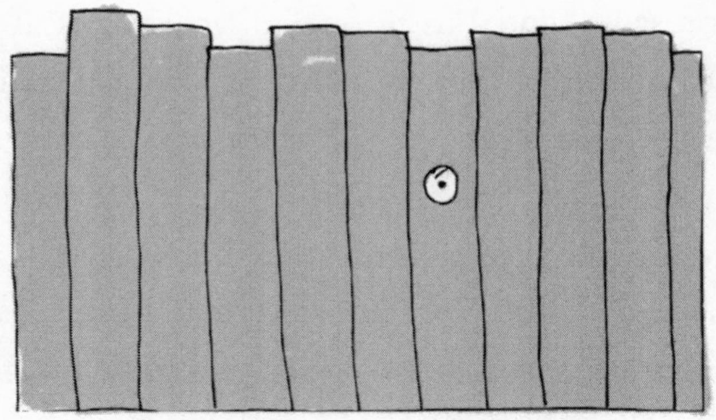

"Melanie and Millicent, the two girls next door to you," says the voice.

"What's wrong with that?" I whisper.

"I'm sure you'll find out soon enough," came the mysterious response.

I didn't know what to say. I felt uncomfortable kneeling on the damp ground and having a conversation with an eyeball about two sisters I'd never met. I don't get the chance to respond, I hear the faint voice of someone calling the name Keira.

"I've gotta go," says the eyeball and then it vanishes.

14:00 PM

I decide to take a walk around the town to see if there was anything interesting about. I manage to find what will be my new school, a library and a few local shops but other than that, it seems pretty desolate. I was close to home and rounding a corner when I walked straight into eyeball-girl.

"Oh hi. Nice to meet you in person. I'm Georgie," I say offering my hand for her to shake.

"Keira," she replies, looking away shyly.

"Are you ok?" I ask. "You always seem a little scared to talk or something."

Keira shakes her head. "I just need to get back home before Melanie and Millicent see me."

Wow this girl was either super-paranoid or was having a really rough time of it. "Why, what are they going to do?"

"What aren't they going to do," replies Keira with sadness. "They're always picking on me and because they're so popular, nobody ever says anything to them. I hate school, I hate living so close to them and I hate them."

Poor Keira! She looks as though she's about to burst into a million tears, which is slightly uncomfortable when you've only just met someone. I rack my brains to try and think of something supportive and nice to say but my mind is raging. If there's one thing I hate more than anything – it's a bully! I detest bullies. They're cruel and spiteful cowards.

Keira looks at the ground and shuffles her feet and I finally manage to think of something to say to her when I hear the stomp of someone walking and two girls come into view. Straight away you can tell that they're twins and the sinking sensation in my stomach tells me that they are the illusive Melanie and Millicent.

"Looky what we we've got here Millie," says the other girl, which using the power of deduction is obviously Melanie.

"Ooooh – Keira's got a new friend," says Melanie.

"I wonder if she's as stupid as her," says Millicent.

The two girls continue to systematically hurl insults towards me and Keira. I stand my ground and look as defiant as I can with my arms crossed, leaning my weight on one foot. Keira on the other hand is struggling to lift her head, and her eyes are darting anywhere but to the faces of these two horrible devilish twins. Anger begins to swell inside – just who did these two think they were? I put my hands deep into my coat pockets and I feel my fingers grip my wand. I know that I can't cast in public – mom would be furious if we had to move again so soon, but there my temper is flaring. Out the corner of my eye I see a large dog strolling with its owner on the other side of the road. My hand shakes and grips my wand tighter as I listen to the terrible-twosome continue their verbal attack on me and Keira.

"Love the hair as well," Millicent says to me. "Haven't you heard of straighteners?"

Melanie starts to cackle and gives an approving nod to her sister. I'm holding my wand so tightly that my knuckles are starting to hurt. The dog is minding its own business with its leg cocked in the air as it relieves itself on a tree. My eyes flit from the dog to the twins – from the twins to Keira – and finally back to the dog. The fury inside me bubbles to the surface and before

I have time to stop myself, I remove the wand from my pocket and flick it out towards the dog.

The dog across the street lowers its leg and stares at Melanie and Millicent. It starts to tug violently against the leash and tugs it from the hands of its owner.

"Benton!" screams the owner.

Benton bounds across the street, barking deeply and begins to snarl aggressively at Melanie and Millicent. The two girls jump back and hold on to each other as Benton edges nearer, stands on its back legs and knocks the twins to the ground and into a great big muddy puddle.

"Arrrghhhhhhh!" the twins scream.

Benton's owner rushes over and secures his dog again. "Sorry girls – he's never done anything like that before!"

Tears are streaming down Melanie's and Millicent's mud caked faces.

I quickly pocket my wand again. I'm in complete and utter shock! I cast a spell – no wait, I cast a spell and it worked! Thankfully it appears that both Melanie and Millicent were too preoccupied with their cruel taunts to actually notice me brandish my wand. I look over to Keira, she's staring at me with wide-eyes, mouth agape and I know instantly that she saw everything.

"You – you," stutters Keira.

I grab her by the arm and walk towards my house, leaving Melanie and Millicent blubbing in their mud bath. When we're far enough away from them, I stop walking and face Keira.

"Listen," I say. "Whatever you think you saw – you didn't."

As explanations go it was a pretty rubbish one but I couldn't think of anything else.

"I think I saw you use a wand to get that dog to attack Melanie and Millicent," replies Keira.

I shake my head and adopt the best look of fake surprise that I could. "Please – that is the most ridiculous thing I ever heard."

"Empty your pockets then," Keira says to me bluntly.

Now I adopt the 'how very dare you' look but I can see from Keira's unconvinced expression, that I wasn't fooling her.

I sigh and plonk myself down on a tree stump in defeat. Mom is really, really going to flip when she finds out that I've already blown our cover! I can just see her disapproving glare as she's repacking the boxes. There's nothing for it – I need to take matters into my own hands; I think adults call it damage limitation. I look at Keira – she's watching me with curiosity. Here we go!

"Keira," I whisper, looking around to make sure that the coast is clear. "Can you keep a secret?"

Coming Soon

The Diary of a Rubbish Witch
SCHOOL
2 New Girl
By Natalie Bailey

After something different?
Why not check out these other great stories by Natalie Bailey!

Jack is just a normal kid, doing normal kid things, until a simple homework project reveals a centuries-old mystery. Can Jack and best friend Charlie, solve the riddle and stop the evil bogeymen in their tracks? Maybe with the help of Charlie's crazy nan, they might just stand a chance. Or maybe, everything might not be what it seems.....

James Mason's life was great; until his Dad got married that is. Now his horrible stepmother - Esmeralda, seems intent on making his life a misery. She's even written a letter to Santa Claus, telling him just how naughty James has been. Not that James is bothered. Santa doesn't even exist, does he?

About the Author

Natalie Bailey lives in Birmingham, England with her long-suffering husband and eight year old son. When she's not busy writing, Natalie spends her spare time wrestling brown bears, swimming with sharks and back-flipping all around the back garden (oh – and telling big fat porky-pies!)

Printed in Great Britain
by Amazon.co.uk, Ltd.,
Marston Gate.